Hey Jack!

The New Friend
first published in 2012
this edition published in 2017 by
Hardie Grant Egmont
Ground Floor, Building 1, 658 Church Street
Richmond, Victoria 3121, Australia
www.hardiegrantegmont.com.au

A CiP record for this title is available from the National Library of Australia

Text copyright © 2012 Sally Rippin
Illustration copyright © 2012 Stephanie Spartels
Logo and design copyright © 2012 Hardie Grant Egmont

Design by Stephanie Spartels
Typesetting by Michaela Stone

Printed in China through Asia Pacific Offset

1 3 5 4 2

Hey Jack!

The New Friend

By Sally Rippin

Illustrated by Stephanie Spartels

hardie grant EGMONT

Grumpy face

Fed up

No-one to play with

Grouchy Mood

Chapter One

This is Jack. Today Jack
is in a grouchy mood.
His best friend Billie
is away and he has
no-one to play with.

'Cheer up, Jack,' says his dad. 'Why don't we play soccer in the park?'

'All right,' says Jack grumpily. Jack's dad isn't very good at soccer. But he is better than no-one.

Jack and his dad kick the ball around the oval.

2

Soon it is time to go
home for dinner.

Jack and his dad walk
back to their house.

Someone **trots**
along behind them.

'Look!' says Jack.

'There is a puppy
following us.'

'So there is,' says Jack's dad. 'I wonder where he came from?'

Jack crouches down.
The puppy runs up to him.

'Hello, little fella,'
says Jack's dad.
'Let's see who you
belong to.'

But the puppy has
no collar, no name
and no address.

A man and a woman
walk towards them,
pushing a pram.

6

'Is this your puppy?'
says Jack's dad.

'No,' says the man.
'We saw him before.
He must be lost.'

Jack's dad **knocks**
on the door of a house
nearby. An old woman
opens the door.

'Is this your puppy?'
Jack's dad asks her.

'No,' says the woman.

'We can't leave him
here on his own,'
Jack says. 'Can't we take
him home with us?'

'Well, I guess it's getting
late,' says Jack's dad.
'We will look after him
tonight. Then tomorrow
we will find his owner.'

9

'Yay!' says Jack.

The puppy **yaps**

excitedly. Jack laughs

and carries him home.

Jack's mum is making dinner. When she sees the puppy she looks very surprised.

'My goodness!' she says. 'Where did he come from?'

'He's lost,' says Jack.

'Don't worry,' says Jack's dad. 'He is only staying one night.'

Jack and his dad
find some old towels.
They make a bed for
the puppy in the laundry.
The puppy turns around
and around in circles.
Then he **flops**
down onto the bed.

Jack sits next to
the puppy.

12

The puppy wriggles
around on his back.
Jack tickles his
soft grey belly.

'If you were my puppy
I would call you Scraps,'
says Jack. He imagines
all the fun that he
and Scraps would
have together.

Chapter Two

Jack's mum comes

into the laundry.

She has a bowl

of water in one hand.

In the other hand

she has a little bowl

of minced meat.

'Here,' says Jack's mum.

'He's probably hungry.'

She puts the bowls down.

The puppy jumps up

and **gobbles**

up all the food.

16

Then he laps at the
water. His little tail spins
around like a propeller.

'He's so cute!' says Jack.

'Can't we keep him?'

'No, Jack,' says his mum.

'He doesn't belong to us.'

'But we already looked for his owner,' Jack says.

Jack's mum shakes her head. 'Imagine if this was your puppy and he went missing?' she says. 'Wouldn't you be sad?'

Jack **sighs** unhappily.

He knows his mum

is right.

'It's time for dinner

now,' Jack's mum says.

'Wash your hands
before you come
to the table.'

After dinner, Jack
goes to say goodnight
to the puppy.
He is curled up on
his bed snoring.
His furry little tummy
moves up and down.

'Good night, Scraps,'

whispers Jack.

Jack's dad tucks him

in to bed.

'Tomorrow morning we'll go see Alf at the corner shop,' he says. 'He might know who the puppy belongs to.'

'All right,' says Jack glumly. 'But if we can't find the owner, can we keep him? Please?'

'We'll see,' says Jack's dad, smiling. 'We'll see.'

Jack lies awake thinking about the puppy. He thinks about his sweet little face and his **waggy** tail.

Just then, Jack hears the puppy whimpering in the laundry.

Jack creeps out of bed.

His parents' bedroom

door is closed.

He tiptoes downstairs

to check on the puppy.

'Hey, Scraps,'

Jack whispers as he

opens the laundry door.

'What's the matter?'

The puppy yaps happily.

'Shhh!' says Jack.
'Mum and Dad will
hear you.' He quickly
closes the door.

Jack pats the puppy.
Scraps **wriggles**
and jumps around.

Jack giggles.

26

'That's enough,' he says.

'It's time for sleep.'

Jack lies down on

the towels.

He closes his eyes

and pretends to sleep.

Soon the puppy snuggles

down next to him.

Jack lies very still.

He will just stay here

until the puppy is asleep…

Suddenly, Jack hears

a voice calling him.

'Jack!' his dad says.

'What are you

doing here?'

Jack can't believe it.

It's morning!

Chapter Three

Jack blinks. 'I...I...
just came to check
on Scraps, I mean,
the puppy,' he says.
'I must have fallen asleep!'

Jack's dad shakes his head and **chuckles**.

'You'd better go and get dressed before Mum sees you.'

The puppy jumps up
and down. Jack picks him
up and gives him a cuddle.
'I'll come back when
I'm dressed,' he says.

'Then we'll go and visit
Alf,' Jack's dad says.
'To see if he knows who
the puppy belongs to.'

After breakfast, Jack
and his dad walk
to Alf's corner shop.
Jack carries the puppy
in his arms. When they
open the shop door,
a bell **jingles**.
Alf comes out of
a room at the back.

'Oh, there you are,

you little scamp!' Alf says

when he sees the puppy.

'I was wondering

where you'd got to!'

Jack gasps. 'You mean

he's *your* puppy?'

'Yep,' says Alf. 'Thanks

for bringing him back.'

35

He holds out his hands
towards the puppy.

Jack looks down at the
puppy in his arms.
He can't believe Scraps
belongs to Alf.
Already he feels like
Jack's puppy.

'Goodbye, Scraps,'
Jack whispers sadly.

The puppy licks Jack's
cheek. Jack hands the
puppy to Alf.

Now Jack just wants
to leave the shop as
quickly as he can.
Tears sting his eyes.

Alf tucks the puppy
under one arm
and sighs. 'You don't
know anyone who'd
like a puppy, do you?
Come look at this!'

Alf pushes open the door
to the back room.

There, lying on a rug,
is a big grey dog.
Rolling all around her
are one, two, three, four
little puppies!

'What on earth am I
going to do with
five puppies?' Alf says.

Jack feels his heart
begin to beat **wildly**.
He looks up at
his dad, full of hope.

'Well, I can think
of a home for one
of those little pups,'
Jack's dad says. 'What
do you reckon, Jack?'

'Oh yes, thank you, Dad!' Jack says, hugging him tightly.

Scraps yaps happily.

'But no more sleeping
in the laundry, OK?'
his dad adds.

Jack grins and shakes
his head. He feels like
the luckiest boy alive.